RUSSELL HOBAN

Illustrated by Toni Goffe

MACDONALD YOUNG BOOKS

Chapter 1

There was a little family of monsters and their name was Scalybum, Mum and Dad and Robert. They lived far away in the mountains. They had a monster TV and when there was nothing on TV they hired videos. They watched *Jumboola* and *The Return of Jumboola*. They watched *Bride of Jumboola, Jumboola Strikes Back* and *Bride of Jumboola's Vengeance*.

Dad never missed a monster film but he thought most of them were not very good. "They do not even use real monsters," he said. "Those are only little dolls."

One evening after they had watched *Jumboola Strikes Back Again* for the ninth time Dad said, "Robert could do better than that with our camcorder."

"What is her name?" said Mum.

"I do not know," said Robert.

"I think Melodina is a very pretty name," said Mum. "Did you have anyone in mind for the part?"

"I thought maybe you could do it," said Robert.

"I will sing but I will not dance," said Mum. "I draw the line at dancing."

"No dancing," said Robert. "Melodina loves to wander in the mountains picking flowers and singing. There is a monster composer spending a few weeks in the mountains."

"Rodolfo would be a good name for him," said Dad.

"Rodolfo is in the mountains because nobody liked the last thing he composed," said Robert. "His doctor told him he should get away from everything and have a good rest.

"One day Rodolfo hears Melodina singing. He gets all excited and he follows the sound, leaping from rock to rock. Then he sees her and he falls in love with her."

"That is nice," said Mum, "I like that."

"I hope there is going to be some action," said Dad.

"There is action coming," said Robert. "Melodina does not know that Rodolfo has seen her and he is too shy to say hello. He follows her around and he writes music."

"He is inspired," said Mum. "Melodina inspires him."

"Right," said Robert. "He is writing Melodina music."

"A symphony," said Mum. "His Melodina symphony."

"We hear that music when he looks at Melodina," said Dad.

"But now there is other music," said Robert. "Here come some people vans. On the sides of the vans it says SCUM."

"A rock group?" said Dad.

"Heavy metal," said Robert. "They are in the mountains to make a video."

"Under their music we can still hear the Melodina symphony music," said Dad. "That is how they do it in films."

"Melodina is still picking flowers and singing," said Robert, "and the SCUM lead singer and guitarist hears her."

"Oh, dear," said Mum.

"He follows the sound of her voice and he sees her," said Robert. "He tells her he can take her away from all this and make her rich and famous."

"Where is Rodolfo?" said Dad. "What is the matter with him?"

"He is busy writing his music," said Robert. "Melodina says no to the SCUM leader but he runs back to his van and gets a gun with one of those darts that put you to sleep."

"That man is no gentleman," said Mum.

"I saw this coming as soon as I heard the name of the group," said Dad.

"He wants to put Melodina on stage in a great big cage," said Robert.

"Melodina will never sing for him in a cage," said Mum.

"Melodina is running away up the mountain and the SCUM lead guitarist is running after her," said Robert.

"Then he stops and he says, 'If you will not sing for me you will not sing for anybody.' The band starts playing as hard as they can and he tells his sound man to turn up the volume."

"I know what is coming," said Dad.

"On the mountain above Melodina," said Robert, "we can see some little rocks rolling down, then some bigger ones."

"Oh, no," said Mum.

"Rockslide," said Dad.

"Now it looks as if the whole top of the mountain is sliding down towards Melodina," said Robert. "But Rodolfo sees what is happening."

"Under the roar of the rockslide and the crashing of the SCUM music we hear the Melodina symphony music getting stronger," said Dad.

"Come on, Rodolfo!" said Mum.

"Here he comes," said Robert. "He throws down his notebook and he is leaping from rock to rock. He is trying to get to Melodina before the rockslide does."

"Go, Rodolfo!" said Dad.

"Save Melodina!" said Mum.

"Rodolfo grabs Melodina," said Robert. "He leaps to safety with her in his arms. The rockslide goes thundering down the mountain and the SCUM lead guitarist is standing in its path."

"I cannot look," said Mum.

"He brought it on himself," said Dad.

"But wait," said Dad. "Rodolfo has got a coil of rope over his shoulder. He was going to do a little mountain-climbing before this happened. He throws one end of the rope to the SCUM lead guitarist and saves him too."

Mum was crying. "You will play Rodolfo," she said to Dad.

"I will do my best," said Dad.

"Now the SCUM vans are moving out," said Robert. "They drive slowly down the mountain."

"Rodolfo takes Melodina in his arms," said Mum. "He tells her how she inspired him, he tells her how he loves her."

"And the Melodina symphony music comes up very strong for the ending," said Dad.

"Do you think my story will make a good film?" said Robert.

"I think it is wonderful," said Mum. "What will you call it?"

"*Melodina Symphony* is the only name for it," said Dad.

"Right," said Robert. "How do we do the people and the vans and all that?"

"We will use dolls for the people and models for the vans and the rest of the people gear," said Dad.

"It sounds like a lot of work," said Robert.

"It will be worth it," said Dad. "With this film I think we could break into the monster-film business.

Chapter 3

Mum and Dad and Robert worked for months on the dolls and the models. Dad bought a book that told them how to make it look as if the dolls and the models were moving. It was very hard to do.

Then came the Melodina and Rodolfo part of the film. Robert worked the camcorder and Mum and Dad did the acting. They had a lot of trouble with the rockslide. They had to do it several times to get it right and it was hard work to carry the rocks back up the mountain each time.

Dad had to buy some new equipment for some of the things they had to do. Then he bought more books that told them how to do those things.

After they did all the voices and put all the parts of the film together Robert wrote the SCUM music and Mum wrote the Melodina symphony music. Then Robert played his music on his electric guitar and Mum played hers on the piano and they put the music on the film.

At last the film was done. Mum and Dad and Robert watched it over and over and Mum cried every time.

"I will send a copy of this to Megafright International," said Dad. "They are the people who make the best monster films. Maybe they will give us a lot of money for it. Maybe they will sign us up to make films for them."

Dad sent *Melodina Symphony* to Megafright International in Peopletown. It came back in two days. There was a letter with it:

Dear Mr Scalybum,

Your film is not very good. In fact it is pretty bad. The music is OK and the human actors are all right but anybody can see that the rockslide is a fake and the monsters just do not look real enough.

Faithfully yours,

J. M. Flatbrain,
President,
Megafright
International

"Do not look real enough!" said Dad. "I think I had better have a word with Mr Flatbrain."

"I have heard that Peopletown is not a friendly place," said Mum.

"That is all right," said Dad, "because I do not feel very friendly just now."

"Robert and I will go with you," said Mum, "and I think we should all put on some helicopter repellent." When they had done that the Scalybums set out for Peopletown.

Chapter 4

When Peopletown saw the Scalybums coming there were sirens, whistles, and public announcements. Buildings emptied as everyone tried to leave at once and there were traffic jams on all the roads. Swarms of helicopters came at them but the helicopter repellent repelled them.

"How can anyone live in a place like this?" said Dad as he brushed away missiles and fighter planes.

"I suppose they are used to it," said Mum.

The Scalybums tried to be as careful as they could but they kept getting their feet stuck in traffic jams. When they got them unstuck they could not help knocking over a few buildings.

They also got tangled in all kinds of wires that pulled a lot of other things down.

"Mind where you step," said Mum.

"How do they expect me to see where I'm going if they keep squirting water in my face?" said Dad as he kicked some fire engines out of the way.

The people at Megafright International had not noticed the noise. They were still in their offices. Dad lifted the top off the building and said to the receptionist, "I'd like to see Mr Flatbrain, please."

"We do not need any actors today," said the receptionist without looking up. "Phone us next week."

"I am not an actor," said Dad.

"Oh, no?" said the receptionist.

"I am a monster," said Dad.

"That is what they all say," said the receptionist. "Phone us next week."

"Look at me," said Dad. "This is not a costume. I am not an actor."

The receptionist looked at Dad and Mum and Robert. "Have a seat, please," she said. They all sat down on a nearby building. "What is your name?" she said.

"Scalybum," said Dad. "John Scalybum. This is my wife Serafina and this is our son Robert."

"What do you want to see Mr Flatbrain about?" said the receptionist.

"Our film," said Dad, "*Melodina Symphony*."

The receptionist spoke to Mr Flatbrain on the telephone. Then she said to Dad, "He says to send it to him and he will look at it."

“I have done that,” said Dad.

The receptionist spoke to Mr Flatbrain again. Then she said to Dad, “He wants to know if that is the one with the rockslide.”

“That is the one,” said Dad.

The receptionist spoke to Mr Flatbrain again. Then she said to Dad, “Mr Flatbrain says the monsters are just not real enough.”

Dad reached into the office behind the receptionist and picked up Mr Flatbrain. "What about me?" he said. "Am I real enough?"

"Not really," said Mr Flatbrain. "You are pretty real but you will have to get a lot realer if you want to break into the monster business. Try again and let us see your next film."

"Not likely," said Dad. He put Mr Flatbrain down. "I think it is time to go home," he said to Mum and Robert. "I have had enough of this place."

Dad put the top back on the Megafright International building. Then Mum and Dad and Robert tidied up Peopletown as well as they could. Then they went home. When they got their feet up and settled down to watch TV they all felt better.

"Look," said Mum. "There we are on the Six o'Clock News. Why did I wear that hat? *Nobody* is wearing that kind of hat this year. I look awful."

"You look terrific," said Dad. "You always do. Do I look real to you?"

"You will always look real to me," said Mum, "and you will always be my Rodolfo."

"Our film was not a success," said Dad.

"It was fun though," said Robert. "I never really wanted to break into the monster business anyway. Can we watch *Jumboola* tonight?"

"Yes," said Mum and Dad. So they did.

Look out for more titles in the Storybook series:

Dreamy Daniel, Brainy Bert by Scoular Anderson

Daniel is always getting into trouble at school. But with the help of the brainy class mouse, Bert, Daniel learns to beat his day-dreaming habit.

Look Out, Loch Ness Monster! by Keith Brumpton

For as long as he can remember, Kevin McAllister has longed to see the Loch Ness Monster. Then, one dark Scottish night, his dream comes true!

The Twenty Ton Chocolate Mountain by Helen Muir

Mr McWeedie doesn't teach the children much about reading or adding up. Instead, he tells them about spaghetti trees and singing sunflowers – and the Twenty Ton Chocolate Mountain.

Hurray for Monty Ray! by Sam McBratney

Monty Ray has a new baby brother – the sixth boy in the family! Nobody can think of a name for the new baby, so he's just called Lamb Chop. Monty Ray is very worried – what if the name sticks?

Nigel the Pirate by Roy Apps

When Cap'n Bonegrinder knocked on the door asking for apprentice boy pirates, Nigel thought this was his chance to make his mark on the world. But Nigel's hopes were soon sunk on board 'The Bloody Plunderer'.

Tell Tale Tom by Anne Forsyth

Tom is an ordinary black-and-white cat with an extraordinary talent for making up tall tales. His fibs always land him in trouble, until the day that he finds himself the hero of the whole town!

Storybooks can be bought from your local bookshop or can be ordered direct from the publishers. For more information, write to: *The Sales Department, Macdonald Young Books Ltd, Campus 400, Maylands Avenue, Hemel Hempstead HP2 7EZ.*